Once Upon a Rainbow

Pictures by
Gabriele Eichenauer

Story told by Naomi Lewis

Jonathan Cape   Thirty Bedford Square   London

Oh, Teddy, if only the rain would stop!"
Anna took the little bear on her knee and practised again the rhyme that her brother had made her learn. Tom was a year older than Anna and was always teaching her what he called Useful Facts; he was very severe if she didn't remember. This time it was about the proper order of colours in a rainbow.

> "Red, orange, yellow, green
> (No one has ever seen
> Since a rainbow first began
> A rainbow of a different plan.)
> Next comes blue – and don't forget
> The last two colours of the set :
> Indigo, then violet."

"What's indigo?" she had asked him. But he had rushed off without telling her.

A ray of sunlight struck the room. Anna looked out.

"Teddy!" she cried, and held up the little bear. "There's a rainbow, and it reaches right up to our wall. I do believe we could walk on it. Come along!"

Still holding Teddy, she slid out of the window on to the flower-bed just below. The rainbow was certainly there. She set one foot on it cautiously, then the other. She might have been treading on coloured snow.

At the highest point of the arch she stopped. The rainbow trembled; it began to dissolve around her. In her fright she closed her eyes – how glad she was to have Teddy! When at last she dared to look she saw that she was standing in a great circular rainbow with a shining centre. Where it shone the grass was green and marvellous flowers grew. Everywhere else was wild and bleak – a sweeping plain with bare rocky hills.

And then she saw before her something – someone – she would remember all her life. This was a lady of magical beauty, her long hair twined with flowers. Through the folds of her dress strange creatures peered with bright inquiring eyes.

"I am the Rainbow Fairy. Once every seven years a moment comes when a child of seven, born under a rainbow, recites the seven rainbow colours in the proper order. You are such a child and now you may visit the seven Rainbow Lands. There is one condition: a rhyme brought you here and a rhyme must be your pass before you can leave each country for the next. You look alarmed; there is no need. Now you may ask one question."

"Please," said Anna, "what is indigo? I asked Tom, but he didn't stay to tell me."

"Darker than blue; bluer than total dark – that is Indigo. Now, Scarlet," – she lifted a butterfly on her finger – "take this child to Red Land, and see that others know about her coming."

There was a rainbow mist, then nothing, only the butterfly, where the fairy had been.

Anna picked up Teddy and ran after the butterfly. But it fluttered in all directions, as butterflies do, and soon was out of sight. She looked around. There was no doubt where she was. Red Land! Waving poppies grew in thousands. The sky was tinged with red as if it reflected a fire. A warm wind ruffled her hair. It seemed to speed a group of children running towards her, all of them holding kites on very long strings. The kites looked just like huge scarlet butterflies.

"You've come!" said the nearest child. "We have a kite for you too. But first you must tell us your Red Land rhyme. We long for new words to sing. Please say it now."

To her surprise, Anna found herself reciting lines that she did not know she knew.

> *"A ladybird, a pillar-box,*
> *Sometimes a squirrel or a fox,*
> *A rose hip or a rose,*
> *Geranium and pimpernel,*
> *The butterfly Red Admiral,*
> *Ripe strawberries, the best of all —*
> *What is more red than those?"*

"We don't know all those things but they sound just right," said the child. "That's a specially good line about the butterfly. Now here's your kite. Remember – it can't go over the Red Land border."

Anna settled herself on the butterfly-kite. The children waved and sang lines of the poem over and over again. Teddy held on behind, and up they went. It was lovely . . .

Then the kite would go no further, and it tipped them off.

They dropped on to a cloud. Almost at once they were gently lifted down.

"Only a giant", Anna thought, "could have reached so far." And a giant it was. She could see that his clothes, eyes and hair were of a rich orange-tawny colour. She looked around. There was a flame-like glow in the sky. The hills and fields and river shone with the same light.

"Sunset changes to sunrise in Orange Land," said the giant, "then sunrise back to sunset. You can't stay here long, I'm sorry to say, but I would like to hear your rhyme. You have one, I suppose?"

"Well, yes," said Anna, "I have. It's about the things at home that could be in Orange Land."

"Such as . . . ?"

> *"Tangerine,*
> *Clementine,*
> *The carrots I grew last year.*
> *Nasturtiums, crocuses,*
> *Apricots, goldfishes,*
> *And my friend Bridget's hair.*
> *Marigolds that never fade,*
> *Oh, yes : our cat called Marmalade . . .*

"I'm afraid the rhyme isn't very good," said Anna, "but nothing rhymes with the things I want to tell you about."

The giant gave a laugh that rumbled off into the hills.

"I think I know most of those," he said. "Some are even embroidered on my jacket. What I *would* rather like is a cat called Marmalade. Company doesn't often come my way. But now you must go to my neighbour – a wonderful fellow. I'll lift you over the border."

His hand was gentle but for Anna it was a dizzy rise and an even dizzier drop. And then she was looking into the face of a great gold-coloured lion. "Welcome, Anna," he said. "I must tell you straight away that the light here is more dazzling than you imagine. You cannot stay long, but we have a little time. Now, what would you think to find in Yellow Land?"

"Yellow Land, desert sand," said Anna, almost to herself. The lion glanced down. Anna did too. Sand was under her feet. Sand was everywhere.

"So!" said the lion. "What next?"

"A tree full of lemons," said Anna.

It was a handsome tree. The lemons shone; their scent filled the air.

"Yes?" the lion said. "And then?"

"Oh ... canary birds," said Anna. She had to think quickly.

Canaries perched on the lemon-tree boughs before flying away again. The lion watched them go.

"We have no cages here," he murmured. "But enough!" He held up his paw. "You must move on to the Green Country. Now if I go too near the border its leaves and grass will shrivel and turn gold; that won't do at all. You have said your poem, by the way – did you realize? Short, but it will do. The sand, remember? Add the lemons and a canary – that should satisfy the fairy. Now here is a magic mirror. Look into it, count seven and you will be in the Green Country."

Anna looked: she counted. As she said "seven" she remembered, just too late. Teddy!

But here she was, in a grassy glade. How fresh and green it was. Even the sky shone green through a roof of leaves. And there before her was a large green bird, a parrot or cockatoo.

"Good, good," said the cockatoo. "You are in good time! Let us hear your rhyme."

"It seems to be a kind of riddle," Anna said doubtfully.

"How does it go? How does it go?" said the cockatoo.

> *"Cress in my window grew,*
> *Mint leaf and parsley too.*
> *Grass blade and grasshopper*
> *And great trees in the forest were.*
> *These were big*
> *And those were small.*
> *The cress grew short; the trees grew tall.*
> *One word belongs to all."*

"I know the answer," said the bird, "it's a colour. Your new dress has it too."

Anna looked. To her surprise she was wearing a beautiful leaf-coloured dress, fine as silk, light as air – a dress for dancing in.

"You wish to dance?" said the cockatoo. "Good, good, now's your chance. I shall sing and you will dance."

It was a strange song but fast in pace and Anna danced and danced. Suddenly she stopped.

"Has a little bear passed through here?" she asked.

"Not that I know. But don't be sad. Don't be blue. As the song goes:

> *If you are sad, if you are blue*
> *The Green Land won't do, won't do.*
> *Blue Country is the place for you."*

As he sang Anna found herself dancing again. Her steps led away from the green green wood . . .

To the Blue Country. It was not a land at all! She was deep down in the sea, just as if she were a mermaid. She might have been still in a forest, with the branching trees and waving plants. But all was blue, though the blue was of more shades than she could have imagined.

And how very odd! There was a real clown, with a clown's sad-funny face; he was juggling with a number of apples, and *they* were a dark shiny blue. He was calling out:

> *"Why am I here? Why am I here?*
> *To keep you in good cheer."*

And that was what he did. All kinds of sea-creatures came to watch – starfish, sea-horses, even an octopus. Anna was so entranced that once again Teddy went right out of her thoughts. The clown stopped.

"Just fancy! I was forgetting! Your poem, Anna . . ."

> *"When I came to Blue Country*
> *Never before*
> *Had I known of such blue.*
> *There were kinds without number.*
> *I tried to remember*
> *The blue things I knew*
> *(There should be quite a few).*
> *First, a blue cornflower,*
> *The jewel called sapphire,*
>
> *Blue bird and kingfisher,*
> *Flax, periwinkle,*
> *Speedwell and bluebell,*
> *The stripes of a mackerel;*
> *Mussel-shell, winkle;*
> *A blue china plate,*
> *Ice, flint and slate.*
> *But on the sea's floor*
> *Are a hundred times more."*

The clown shook her hand.

"You should be a clown, too, with all those notions. Now we have all earned a rest."

The sea turned a deeper blue. Night comes under the sea just as it does on the land. Looking up, Anna saw through the waves the shimmering shape of the moon.

She also saw twinkling stars. They seemed quite close to the water. Strange! She began to swim upwards to have a closer look.

As soon as she reached the surface she understood. The starry lights came from the hair of two fairy creatures hovering over the water.

"We are the Star Children," said one. "We have been waiting for you." They took her hands and they all soared into the midnight sky.

"Ours is the smallest rainbow country," she was told, "and the most mysterious. Darker than blue; bluer than total dark. It disappears each dawn."

"Darker than blue; bluer than total dark" – who had said that? Anna remembered. The Fairy had told her the meaning of indigo. This meant she was almost at the end of her journey. Teddy! Would he be left on the rainbow? But the Star Children were asking for her poem. She began:

> *"Never did I think,*
> *In my bed below,*
> *That the sky which looked like ink*
> *Was really Indigo.*
>
> *Disappearing land!*
> *Shall I ever know,*
> *Shall I ever understand*
> *The country Indigo?"*

A shooting star sped by.

"That means a wish for you, Anna," said the nearest Star Child. "But don't say it aloud. It must be a quite small wish as it is a quite small star. Time is short – we must leave you on a cloud."

As Anna made her wish, their voices died away and the little stars went out.

How comfortable to lie on a cloud! The light in the sky belonged to early dawn, but was strangely tinged with violet. The clouds, the mountain peaks – they all had a violet colour. And – a thrilling sight – so had the fairy-tale castle set on the violet hills. A rhyme came into her mind, and she said it aloud:

"The violet light is magic,
I can't describe its wonder.
Now it looks like lilac,
Now it looks like thunder.
Now it's like an amethyst
Now like thistle flowers.
Maybe I shall find my wish
In those violet towers.

In the land of Violet,
The last in Rainbow order,
One alone has gone inside
But two must reach the border."

At once Anna's cloud began floating along to the castle gates, where it neatly set her down. The great gates opened; she stepped inside and found herself in a high, round hall with many doors, all shut. And there stood the lovely Rainbow Fairy.

"You have nearly finished your journey, Anna. I know what you have wished. But you have to help to make the magic work – and that is true of most wishes. What you have wished for may be in this castle, and yet be somewhere else. Remember: most doors open if you try."

There was a rainbow-coloured mist – then nothing at all. Anna was alone in the hall with the closed doors.

M ost doors open if you try."
Anna thought of the words and went to the nearest door. It opened at her touch. Why, there was the Red Land, with its poppies and butterfly-kites. But the children seemed not to see her. Then the door closed by itself. The next opened on to Orange Land; she looked hard but the giant was alone. Again, the door closed. So she went on, glancing hopefully into each but not seeing what she sought. She reached the seventh. Now here was a puzzle; it showed the violet castle in the violet hills – yet she was *in* that castle.

Well, one more door remained.

"This is the way I must take," she told herself. She put out her hand and the door opened just as the others had done, but it led to her own home, to the room she had left to follow the rainbow.

And there in the window-seat was Teddy. So her wish *had* been granted! But what was he looking at? She could hardly believe her eyes. There was a rainbow reaching right to the garden, just as before. Was it the same rainbow? Had she simply slept and dreamt, or *had* Teddy been left in Orange Land?

"Teddy," she said, "where did you get that orange bow?"

But Teddy said not a word.

First published 1981
Copyright © 1981 by Max and Gabriele Gernhardt-Eichenauer
Text copyright © by Naomi Lewis 1981
Jonathan Cape Ltd, 30 Bedford Square, London WC1

British Library Cataloguing in Publication Data

Lewis, Naomi
Once upon a rainbow
I. Title   II. Eichenauer, Gabriele
823′.914 [J]   PZ7
ISBN 0 224 01842 6

Printed in Italy by
New Interlitho, SpA, Milan
Filmset by Keyspools Ltd, Golborne, Lancashire